Disney FROZEN

A Day in the Sun

By Frank Berrios

A Random House PICTUREBACK® Book
Random House 🏠 New York

Copyright © 2014 Disney•Pixar. All rights reserved. Published in the United States by Random House Children's Books, a division of Random House LLC, 1745 Broadway, New York, NY 10019, and in Canada by Random House of Canada Limited, Toronto, Penguin Random House Companies, in conjunction with Disney Enterprises, Inc. Pictureback, Random House, and the Random House colophon are registered trademarks of Random House LLC.

ISBN 978-0-7364-3088-3
randomhouse.com/kids
Printed in the United States of America
10 9 8 7 6 5 4 3 2

Hi! My name is Olaf. I am a snowman, but I've always dreamed about summer!

The blue skies and white clouds!
Buzzing bees and dandelions!
A day in the sun would be so amazing!

At the beach, I could really work on my snowman tan!

Ahoy! I could go sailing! Ahhh, what a lovely breeze!

There's nothing more relaxing than a nice swim!
All my cares would just melt away. . . .

Summertime is also perfect for meeting new friends!

Winter is fine for penguins and ice . . .

. . . but a tap-dancing seagull is twice as nice!

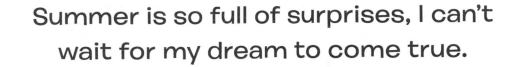

Summer is so full of surprises, I can't wait for my dream to come true.

And then I can play with someone like you!

Crazy for Summer

© Disney

I love HEAT

© Disney